MONSTER MATER

Adapted by Frank Berrios

Random House 🏠 New York

Materials and characters from the movie *Cars*. Copyright © 2006, 2011 Disney/Pixar. Disney/Pixar elements © Disney/Pixar, not including underlying vehicles owned by third parties: H-1 Hummer is a trademark of General Motors. All rights reserved. Published in the United States by Random House Children's Books, a division of Random House, Inc., 1745 Broadway, New York, NY 10019, and in Canada by Random House of Canada Limited, Toronto. Random House and the colophon are trademarks of Random House, Inc.

ISBN: 978-0-7364-2784-5   www.randomhouse.com/kids   MANUFACTURED IN CHINA

3-D special effects by Red Bird Press.   All rights reserved.   10 9 8 7 6 5 4 3

Lightning McQueen and Mater were relaxing at Flo's Café when they saw a monster truck roll by on huge tires.

"I used to wrestle trucks bigger than that," said Mater as he began his story. "Yep, I used to be a Monster Truck Wrestler!"

The lights dimmed in the arena. When Mater and I-Screamer, the monster ice cream truck, entered the wrestling ring, the crowd went wild!

"I'm going to make you scream!" growled I-Screamer as he came face to face with the tow truck. Mater, who was better known as the Tormentor, was scared, but he had a plan!

"Can I have one double-dip dipstick sundae, please?"
asked Mater.

"Huh? Oh, sure," said a confused I-Screamer.
"That's a very popular flavor."

But when I-Screamer turned around to get the ice cream,
Mater flipped the truck over with his hook—and made his
own sundae!

The referee counted to three and declared Mater the winner!

In the next match, Mater had to wrestle Captain Collision. The camouflaged military truck was a crowd favorite because he had a perfect record— twenty-three wins and no losses!

"Drop and give me twenty!" ordered Captain Collision.
"I'll give you three," replied Mater as he raced forward. He bounced off the ropes and flew right into the military truck. The impact knocked Captain Collision off his big tires and onto his back.
"One, two, three," counted the referee. Mater won again!

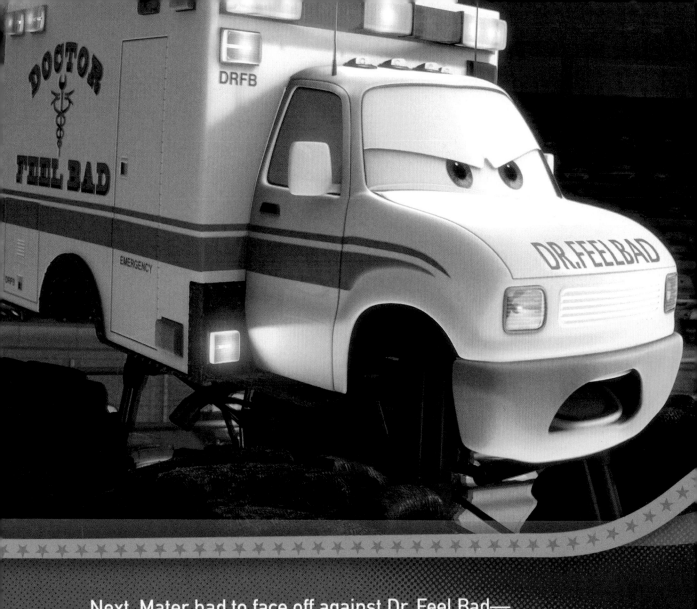

Next, Mater had to face off against Dr. Feel Bad—
the ambulance with an attitude. Fans went wild whenever
Dr. Feel Bad used his wailing sirens to confuse his opponents
before sending them to the emergency room.

"Your next stop is the hospital," warned Dr. Feel Bad as his lights started to flash.

Mater yanked the big-wheeled ambulance against the ropes like a rock in a slingshot—and then let go!

As Dr. Feel Bad flew through the air and out of the stadium, Mater said, "Don't worry . . . I'll bring you some flowers!"

Mater made quick work of his next challenger—
Paddy O'Concrete. Mater used his hook to flip Paddy's cement
mixer. When Paddy tried to cover Mater with cement, it poured
all over Paddy instead!

"Paddy got paved!" cried one fan.

After defeating many challengers, Mater was heading to the big show—the World Championship of Monster Truck Wrestling! Cars from all over the globe had traveled to see the exciting match.

"And now, the moment we've all been waiting for," said the announcer. "The bucktoothed wonder of the world— the Tormentor!"

The crowd cheered wildly as Mater proudly entered the arena.

The crowd started to boo as the evil champ,
Dr. Frankenwagon's Monster, appeared.
   "It's alive!" yelled one fan.
   "I'm dead," Mater said to himself. He had never
faced a wrestler this big and bad!

Lightning interrupted Mater's story. "Whoa, Mater.
You were gonna wrestle that . . . thing?"

"Don't you remember nothin'?" replied Mater. "We was
a tag team."

Sparks flew off Dr. Frankenwagon's Monster as its
cold eyes stared down at Mater and Lightning.

"Tag, you're it!" said Mater, and he swiftly left the ring. Lightning ducked and dodged the Monster's wrecking ball as it chased him around the ring. But before long, Lightning was cornered.

"Quick!" Lightning yelled to Mater. "Tag me, tag me!"

Mater coolly tagged Lightning and snagged the Monster's wrecking ball with his hook. Mater pulled with all his might, flipping the Monster—and the entire ring! Dr. Frankenwagon's Monster smashed to the ground, sending up a huge cloud of dust.

When the dust settled, the Monster was lying on its back. The referee counted to three and declared Mater and Lightning the winners!

"Let's hear it for the new champs—the Tormentor and Frightening McMean!" announced the referee. The crowd cheered!